From Perils *To* Pearls

Dr. Wanda Keele

All Scripture quotations, unless otherwise indicated, are taken from the King James Version (KJV) public domain.

Personal pronouns referring to God (except for "who" or "whom") have been capitalized, to stay consistent with the rest of the text and most importantly, to give honor to the Most High.

"Welcome to Holland" ©1987 by Emily Perl Kingsley. All rights reserved. Reprinted by permission of the author.

Cover design and book layout by Jeff Johnson, www.j2arts.com.

Send all personal correspondence to:
Pastors Dr. Denvil and Dr. Wanda Keele
Provision Ministry
1769 Cedar Avenue, Iuka, Mississippi 38852
Phone: 662-424-9733
Email: wandakeele@yahoo.com

Published by:
Deeper Revelation Books
Revealing "the deep things of God" (1 Cor. 2:10)
P.O. Box 4260, Cleveland, TN 37320
Phone: 423-478-2843
Email: info@deeperrevelationbooks.org
Website: www.deeperrevelationbooks.org

Visit the Deeper Revelation Books website for distribution information and a listing of other products.

Deeper Revelation Books assists Christian authors in publishing and distributing their books. Final responsibility for design, content, permissions, editorial accuracy and doctrinal views, either expressed or implied, belongs to the author.

TABLE OF CONTENTS

FOREWORD

Denvil and Wanda Keele have been dear friends of mine for many years. If I have ever met sincere Christian believers, they are – and their lives show it. That's what this book is all about: showing what real Christianity is, not in complicated terminology you only hear in a Bible college, but the simple words that rise out of a practical, every-day walk of faith. This well-lived kind of life is highly contagious. As you read these stories of tragedy and triumph, major battles and overcoming grace, you will be stirred to react to circumstances in faith too, instead of bowing down to the pressure and giving up.

These precious saints in the LORD have learned – as we all need to – it's not what we face in life that determines who we are, but how we react to what we face. Another couple could have encountered the same negative circumstances and been overwhelmed with depression and discouragement. Faith is a choice; and thankfully, Denvil and Wanda made the decision to walk in faith early on. This wonderful legacy has since been passed to their children, Phillip and April, and their grandchildren, Zackery, Brooklynn and Tanner, as well as Phillip's wife, Elizabeth, April's husband, Bradley, and all those who have met them and learned to love this blessed family. What a rich inheritance!

This inspiring book is called *From Perils to Pearls*. This is a very fitting title, because it's all about God ability to produce good things out of difficult circumstances.

You have to understand how pearls are produced to see the connection. Usually, a parasite or a rough-edged grain of sand enters the folds of an oyster's flesh. The oyster finds this quite irritating, so it does its best to rid itself of this 'uninvited guest.' It opens and shuts many times, creating a current of water that will flush out the 'intruder.' When that fails to work, the oyster does the 'next best thing.'

Over and over – dozens, then hundreds of times – it secretes a milky-like substance called "nacre" (pronounced "NAY-ker"), also known as "mother of pearl." This repeatedly coats the intruding element until it creates something quite beautiful out of something that was initially quite painful. Something very valuable is fashioned which, at the start, seemed to have no value at all.

I am convinced this is why the LORD compares His bride to a "pearl of great price." (See Mt. 13:45-46.) Like an irritating grain of sand, certain uninvited problems, temptations and tribulations enter our lives that we often try to escape through self-effort. When that proves insufficient, we who are saved have learned to 'secrete' out of our hearts another kind of 'milky-like substance': "the sincere milk of the Word" (1 Pt. 2:2).

Over and over again, we 'cover' the battles of life with the commandments and promises found in the Bible. In the process, something very beautiful and valuable is formed in us through the painful experiences of life. The very nature and image of the Jesus Christ takes us over, one layer at a time. In this manner, through the years of serving God, Denvil and Wanda Keele have allowed their hearts and lives to be covered with His Word, day after day, until they succeeded in passing *From Perils to Pearls*.

MIKE SHREVE
Founder of Deeper Revelation Books

INTRODUCTION

According to the Merriam-Webster dictionary, a "peril" is a noun referring to danger by "exposure to the risk of being injured, destroyed or lost." It poses a threat or hazard.

We all face events and circumstances in our lives that cause us to pause, stumble or even fall. However, those same situations can cause us to grow ... if we choose to let them.

In this book, not every challenge endured would fit in the strict definition above – but when we are walking through life, even small things sometimes can throw us off balance and make us feel as if we are under attack or lost.

When the journey does not turn out as we had hoped – when the roads we take turn hazardous – when the risks before us have the ability to end life as we know it and the pain we bear is greater than we think we can endure, it is then that we find out what we are made of. It is during these times in our lives that we reach out for something bigger than ourselves – something with the ability to transform.

It is then that the passage through the perils has the ability to produce a harvest of pearls. Whether we emerge as stronger, more beautiful human beings is up to us. This book is the story of how the Keele's turned their perils into "Pearls of Wisdom."

TERRY JOANN BECK
Editor

*Who shall separate us from the love of Christ? Shall tribulation, or distress, or persecution, or famine, or nakedness, or **peril**, or sword?*

As it is written, for thy sake we are killed all the day long; we are accounted as sheep for the slaughter.

Nay, in all these things we are more than conquerors through Him that loved us.

For I am persuaded, that neither death, nor life, nor angels, nor principalities, nor powers, nor things present, nor things to come.

Nor height, nor depth, nor any other creature, shall be able to separate us from the love of God, which is in Christ Jesus our LORD.

(Romans 8:35-39, emphasis by author)

CHAPTER 1

GOD'S PROTECTION

Mable Keele was a praying woman. She attended church at Poplar Springs Freewill Baptist Church, Iuka, Mississippi, where she often requested prayer for her son, Denvil N. Keele. Denvil was serving in Vietnam. As a mother, Mable cried out to God for protection on Den's behalf. She knew her son was 'lost' – without a personal, saving relationship with Jesus – and did not want him killed while unprepared to meet God. Yet Mable also knew her prayers, and those of her fellow church members, were powerful as they ascended into the heavens and straight to the heart of God.

Denvil served in the infantry division during the Vietnam War. Many times, he had been thrust into danger zones. In his letters back home, Den sometimes wrote about how he had been spared from death.

Staff Sargent Denvil N. Keele, Fort Carson, Colorado, 1975.

One time, in a letter received not long after his mother had requested prayer at church, Den told of an experience while under enemy fire. He had dug a foxhole for himself to seek refuge from the enemy. Suddenly, he experienced a severe stomach cramp and had to be air lifted out. As the helicopter rose above the battle zone, he looked down at his foxhole. His heart sank as he saw that the enemy had wiped out the foxhole he had dug … along with the young man who had replaced him in his position. God had once again caused Den to know 'someone' was watching over him.

Denvil's stomach cramps and constant diarrhea was diagnosed as Crohn's disease. He was also diagnosed with crippling arthritis. Consequently, he was not able to continue his deployment. In addition to his physically disabling symptoms, Den was tormented by nightmares. Nightly, he wrestled with his bed covers while reliving the horrors of war. Den needed healing, comfort and peace, but didn't know the One who could deliver him from his pain and emotional captivity.

PEARL OF WISDOM

"Call unto Me, and I will answer thee, and shew thee great and mighty things, which thou knowest not." (Jeremiah 33:3)

CHAPTER 2
TOUCHED BY GOD

My name is Wanda. Den and I were sweet on each other when we were younger, but both of us too shy to strike up a conversation. I often heard Mable Keele request prayer for her son, Denvil, at the Poplar Springs Church where my family also attended. Like the other church members, I would say a prayer for Den; however, I knew that I was not close enough to God for Him to even hear me.

My parents, Herbert and Dona Johnson, had raised me "right and tight." We lived in Tishomingo, Mississippi; and although it was a small town, I had managed to get myself on the wrong track in life. I married ... and divorced. Like Mable Keele, my parents kept me before the LORD in their prayers.

While Denvil was serving in Vietnam, I was working as the local contact for the Army recruiting office. When Den came home on disability, he was assigned to Tishomingo County as the new United States Army Recruiter. The Army retired Denvil due to his disability in 1977 after approximately seventeen years of service. He was thirty-three years old at the time of discharge. Due

Denvil in full uniform.

to his medical condition, doctors advised him he would not live past the age of forty.

On Friday, May 13, 1977, Denvil felt the convicting power of God calling him to repentance. He came looking for me at my little apartment located across from Cutshall Funeral Home in Iuka, Mississippi. When I answered his knock on the door, I immediately read the conviction on his face. I asked him, "What's troubling you?" He replied, "I don't know." When I asked him if it was the LORD, he said, "Yes." I told him to come into my apartment so we could talk.

Even though I was in a backslidden condition myself at the time, I told Den that I would pray first. You see, I figured I would 'show' him how to repent. Well, I did just that – but when I began praying to God, I ended up really repenting. When I turned around to help Den, to my surprise, he had figured out how to repent by listening to me pray and had already begun his own prayer of repentance. When he was done, I asked him if he felt better. He responded, "Yes! The burden is gone!"

He was so excited about his God encounter that he immediately wanted to tell his parents about it. Den headed back to his home in Leedy, Mississippi. That night, he didn't wrestle with his blankets. For the first time in a very long time, Den slept peacefully in one place on his bed all night long. Glory to God! When he awoke the next morning, he was amazed at the peace he had experienced.

He quietly meditated about this new blessing. Den concluded that if God could cause that kind of peace to come to him, he believed God would also heal him. He began to study the Scriptures and discovered how Jesus had healed during His lifetime. Then he discovered that Jesus is still the same yesterday, today and forever. He resolved, "If Jesus ever healed, then he can still heal today."

At that time, Den was taking forty pills per day for his medical conditions. He started believing God to heal his body. Within two weeks, Den had discontinued taking all of the pills – he was completely healed. (Since this healing, Den has had a few bad times, but nothing serious.)

PEARL OF WISDOM

Jesus Christ the same yesterday, and today and forever. (Hebrews 13:8)

CHAPTER 3

NEW LIFE

As the days passed, each of our newfound relationships with the LORD grew deeper and more passionate. So also did our love for each other. It was on a beautiful day, June 23, 1977, when Denvil and I were joined together in matrimony in Corinth, Mississippi, in the home of Phil and Joan Bingham.

Denvil and Wanda Keele, married June 23, 1977.

Denvil was thirty-three years of age and I was thirty-two. We desired a family of at least two children, a boy and a girl. We bought a fabric shop in Burnsville, Mississippi. It would provide a perfect place to work while raising a family.

On July 28, 1978, in Magnolia Hospital, Corinth, Mississippi, the desire of our hearts was fulfilled. God blessed us with a "big ole" eight pound, four ounce bouncing baby boy. Happiness filled the room.

The delivery doctor brought the baby to Den and me. She just kind of pitched him on my

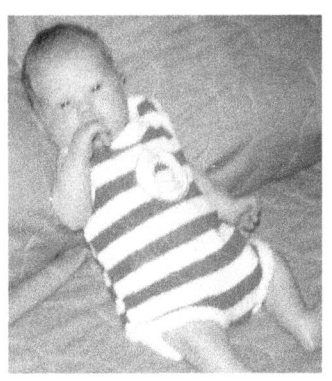

Phillip Den Keele at 4 weeks old.

bed and said, "Does he look normal to you?" We checked our baby over. He had everything we expected to see. I replied, "Everything is in its rightful place – two eyes, two ears, a nose, a mouth, two hands, two feet and … male. All look great as far as I can see." Den confirmed, "He is the most precious thing we have ever seen."

The doctor countered, "I recognize symptoms of Down's syndrome." I answered back, "I don't know what that means." The doctor replied, "Mongoloid." Again, I responded, "I still don't know what that means." The doctor tried once more and said, "Mentally retarded." I remained unaware about the message this doctor was trying to tell me. She went on to say, "Your baby will not be trainable. He will not be able to hold down a job. He will not be able to marry, nor will he bear children. And, he may not walk until he is older. He will be slow to develop in all areas." The doctor and other staff at the hospital offered no hope for his future*.

---

*Down's syndrome is a genetic disorder characterized by a broad skull, blunt facial features, short stature, and learning difficulties. It is caused by the presence of an extra copy of a specific chromosome. (Encarta Dictionary, "Down's syndrome" definition accessed May 16, 2011, http://encarta.msn.com/dictionary_561503882/Down_syndrome.html)

PEARL OF WISDOM

Wherefore they are no more twain, but one flesh. What therefore God hath joined together, let not man put asunder. (Matthew 19:6)

CHAPTER 4

BREAKING THE MOLD

We felt as though our hearts had been stabbed, pierced through to their very core. Tears began to flow. In the midst of the tears, I cried, "I believe God has given us this baby and we are going to love him with all we have." Den stood in total agreement.

The doctor proceeded to inform us about a home in Washington, D.C. that would accept our 'big ole boy' and take care of him until his inevitable death, typically around age eight. Our hearts were broken even more – giving our baby to strangers and never seeing him again – it was unthinkable.

We declined his suggestion to institutionalize our son. Den prayed, "God, he is my son, I love him. LORD, if you heal him – or even if you don't – I will love him the same." Little did we know at the time, we were part of a new breed of parents breaking the mold – no longer choosing to institutionalize our children with Down's syndrome.

We decided to name him Phillip Den. Den was after his dad, of course. Phillip was after a good friend, Phillip Bingham, who showed so much determination in overcoming a swimming accident that had left him paralyzed as a child. He graduated from high school, attended college and became a schoolteacher. Phil was living his life to the fullest in spite of his wheelchair.

Denvil dismissed himself to leave as soon as he felt the baby and I were okay for him to go. He travelled to Happy Holler community, a suburb of North Crossroads, Mississippi, to our little cottage on the hill. There, he poured out his heart to God concerning our baby boy. He dropped down on his knees and earnestly prayed until God gave him perfect peace.

Upon returning to the hospital, Denvil proceeded to encourage me. He was certain that everything was going to be all right. He explained his prayer-time experience to me, "The burden I carried – it just flew away." Now, he was ready for the challenge; and he was prepared to help me through it too.

The doctor discharged us to travel to LeBonner Hospital in Memphis, Tennessee, to confirm his findings. This second report confirmed Phillip had an extra chromosome in the twenty-first set of cells, the definitive medical identification for Down's syndrome. They also pointed out other symptoms typical with Down's syndrome: lower than average IQ, smaller skull, extra folds of skin under the eyes and a flattened nose bridge. The first doctor had correctly diagnosed Phillip.

The doctors at LeBonner educated us even further regarding Phillip's condition. They told us that pneumonia was the number one killer in children with Down's syndrome. They also told us that

Phillip, excited "just because" at age 1.

these children were prone to heart and lung problems. Then, they proclaimed that he would most likely not live past eight years of age.

That was not the report we had hoped for – not the one we had prayed for. Yet, we needed to know all we could about Phillip's condition in order to stand guard on his behalf in the natural, as well as in the spiritual realm.

We left LeBonner Hospital and returned home with Phillip. Things were pretty normal until the latter part of December, 1978, and the first part of January, 1979. It was at that time that congestion set in on Phillip's chest and nose, causing his temperature to rise. The deadly threat of pneumonia lurked in the back of my mind and I knew we must avoid it if at all possible.

We traveled to the emergency room at Iuka Hospital only to find the staff there to be NO help at all. The intern on duty told us to take Phillip home and give him Tylenol. I felt like my heart plummeted down in my shoes. Nevertheless, we brought Phillip home – and not having any other direction – we gave him Tylenol.

Denvil sought the LORD in prayer. I laid Phillip down in the handsome bassinet I had prepared for him and got down on my knees beside him. I began to pray to a living God. I cried out to the same God that had touched Den with healing. I promised God that if He would let our baby live, I would live for Him the rest of my life and do whatever He wanted me to do.

Needless to say, there was not much physical rest that night for Den or me. Yet, at the rising of the sun the next morning, Phillip's fever was gone! The congestion had broken up and he was much, much better. We knew our God had showed up in our lives again with his miracle working power.

We believed that what God had performed for Den, He would surely also accomplish in our baby. We coupled our prayers together with 'walking the Word' and purposed in our hearts to overcome this massive giant that had so vastly interrupted our dreams and our family's life path. We found Jesus to be our one and only source of help.

When Phillip was born, all of our plans had to change. I was afraid to leave Phillip with anyone else. Yet, I was not sure how to raise him myself either. I was mentally exhausted from just getting through the days and nights.

The following short article helps explain how our lives changed; we had landed in a "different place."

Wanda holding baby Phillip, June 1979.

PEARL OF WISDOM

"Walk in the whole Word of God. Amen!"
Dr. Wanda Keele

WELCOME TO HOLLAND
by Emily Perl Kingsley

I am often asked to describe the experience of raising a child with a disability – to try to help people who have not shared that unique experience to understand it, to imagine how it would feel. It's like this ...

When you're going to have a baby, it's like planning a fabulous vacation trip – to Italy. You buy a bunch of guide books and make your wonderful plans. The Coliseum. The Michelangelo David. The gondolas in Venice. You may learn some handy phrases in Italian. It's all very exciting.

After months of eager anticipation, the day finally arrives. You pack your bags and off you go. Several hours later, the plane lands. The stewardess comes in and says, "Welcome to Holland."

"Holland?!?" you say. "What do you mean Holland?? I signed up for Italy! I'm supposed to be in Italy. All my life I've dreamed of going to Italy."

But there's been a change in the flight plan. They've landed in Holland and there you must stay.

The important thing is that they haven't taken you to a horrible, disgusting, filthy place, full of pestilence, famine and disease. It's just a different place.

So you must go out and buy new guidebooks. And you must learn a whole new language. And you will meet a whole new group of people you would never have met.

It's just a different place. It's slower-paced than Italy, less flashy than Italy. But after you've been there for a while and you catch your breath, you look around ... and you begin to notice that Holland has windmills ... and Holland has tulips. Holland even has Rembrandts.

But everyone you know is busy coming and going from Italy ... and they're all bragging about what a wonderful time they had there. And for the rest of your life, you will say "Yes, that's where I was supposed to go. That's what I had planned."

And the pain of that will never, ever, ever, ever go away ... because the loss of that dream is a very very significant loss.

But ... if you spend your life mourning the fact that you didn't get to Italy, you may never be free to enjoy the very special, the very lovely things ... about Holland.

CHAPTER 5

HUNGER FOR GOD

Den surrendered to the ministry call on his life. We worked in a little church called Mount Zion in the North Crossroads community for about nine months. We both knew when God put this in place in our lives, it would soon also be in our ministry.

We moved Den's double-wide trailer onto an acre of property that we purchased from his parents in the Happy Holler community. There, Den found himself a place to pray under a big tree behind our house.

Denvil's prayer tree.

One time in particular, after he had been praying under that big tree, he came into the house and proceeded to ask me to examine his hands. I looked, and to my surprise, they were quite red. I told Den "I don't know what I am looking at." He said that the Spirit of the LORD spoke to his spirit and that He was giving him the gift of healing in his hands. I had never heard of anyone having such thing in my Freewill Baptist Church upbringing. I shrugged my shoulders and told him he better not tell anyone in our circle of friends about what God had spoken to him. They already thought we were strange because Den quit all of his old bad habits and didn't even cuss anymore.

Later, during another special time of talking with the Master under the same old tree in the backyard, the POWER of the HOLY GHOST shook Den so hard that his knees beat their imprint into the ground.

Den was so hungry for whatever God had. He asked me to go with him to Brother Wallace South's church in Corinth, Mississippi. He wanted the baptism of the Holy Ghost. I made him to understand that I did not believe that there was a second work of the Spirit of God. After all, my daddy believed we got everything the first trip. In my eyes, my daddy was the smartest man on the earth. He was the son of a Freewill Baptist minister. Even though I told Den I didn't believe in the baptism of the Holy Ghost for today, I assured him that I would go with him. I also promised that if he received it, I would watch him – and if it was real – I would try it.

Sure enough, that Sunday morning, Den decided to receive this great experience. Brother South asked if someone would come up front and stand proxy for a sick brother of the church. Den heard his door open to receive the baptism of the Holy Ghost.

He did not hesitate for a moment. He slipped out from between the pews, took to the altar and raised his big old, long arms up to Jesus. I did not want to hinder him. As I stood there in our pew, I began to pray and tell God, "I don't believe this; but please don't let me hinder him from receiving." I had my eyes closed. When I opened my eyes, I looked for Den. To my surprise, he was on the floor just jabbering in another language.

One morning, a few weeks later, Den came into the

house. I did not ask him what he had been doing, but told him I had a headache. He immediately placed his hand on my forehead without speaking a word out loud. Instantly my pain was gone!

Another time I specifically remember my lower abdomen was restricted from child labor. Den placed his hand on my stomach area and immediately my discomfort left. Later, Den asked me how my pain was. To my surprise, I had to admit, I had no more pain. GLORY TO GOD! These were my first lessons in training for the ministry.

WOW! I was not acquainted with any of these manifestations of the Holy Ghost. The Holy Ghost was an open door to all the gifts and fruits of the Spirit. Remember, I was the one who had been a church member all those years. Den was the heathen, never claiming to be anything. Now, he's the believer, running after all that God had for him. Sure, I was counted among the daily bible readers in church. And yet, I had wasted so much time. Den was far ahead of me in his relationship with God.

PEARL OF WISDOM

But seek ye first the kingdom of God, and His righteousness; and all these things shall be added unto you. (Matthew 6:33)

CHAPTER 6

A WONDERFUL LIFE

When Phillip was eleven months old, I became pregnant again. During my seventh month of pregnancy, we heard that a man of God named Brother Don James was ministering in the old National Guard Armory building in Iuka, Mississippi, with Brother R.C. and Dorothy Wigginton.

We decided to attend the meeting. Brother Don James was operating under a prophetic anointing. Up until this point, Den and I had witnessed the power of prophecy only one other time in our lives. A prophet once prophesied to Den that God was going to use him in a mighty way – one that would astonish even his family. Brother Don James headed our direction, stopped directly in front of me and declared, "When men look upon the thing in your womb, they are going to recognize that God has touched it and they will know that God is God."

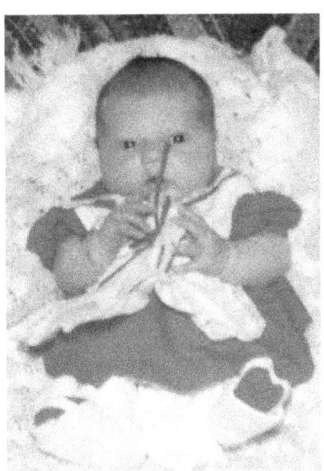

April Sue Keele, 3 weeks old, wearing her body brace.

Like clockwork, two months later, on March 12, 1980, April Sue Keele was born, weighing in at nine pounds two ounces. She was just what we wanted. Our beautiful baby girl had arrived and she looked perfect! We were well on our journey to a wonderful life.

Or, so we thought. Upon examining her, the doctor found her hips were not in place as they should be. Oh, it would have been very easy to accuse God of so many things. After all, what were we facing now? Didn't we already have enough to deal with? Why LORD? Nevertheless, we stood firm and believed that God could fix anything.

We called our friend, Martha Oxendine, to come to the hospital and pray for our baby. We had heard that Martha had the gift of healing in her hands. When she came into the hospital room, the power of God filled the area with a heavy, thick fog. Hallelujah! We were confident everything was going to be all right. Our prayers would not go unnoticed by our living God. He who began a good work would be faithful to complete it!

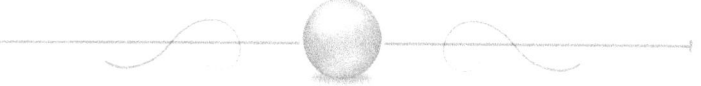

PEARL OF WISDOM

For I reckon that the sufferings of this present time are not worthy to be compared with the glory which shall be revealed in us. (Romans 8:18)

CHAPTER 7
BRACING FOR THE FUTURE

The doctor would not let us leave the hospital without placing a brace on April. He also scheduled an appointment for our baby at LeBonner Hospital in Memphis, Tennessee. It was during that visit to LeBonner that the prayer we had offered up on April's behalf manifested. The doctor there could not pop her hips out of their sockets. He tried repeatedly until he made April cry out. Den stepped forward and said, "That's enough pressing on her hips."

We recalled the story in the Bible concerning the woman with the issue of blood. The Scripture stated that she had suffered many things at the hands of doctors. Sometimes professionals, in the natural, cause much pain to God's people as they try to be medically 'right'.

On the way home, Den said to me, "Momma, the LORD has let me see that we need to remove those braces now. Otherwise, the doctors will want to break her little legs to put her feet back in front of her."

I began to weep. I couldn't agree with him at this point. I just couldn't! Fear gripped me. It had suddenly gotten bigger than my faith, though I did not realize it at the time.

We were traveling back to our little cottage in the Happy Holler community in Iuka. As we passed the little country church called Mt. Zion (where Den had surrendered to the ministry and actually pastored for a season before April was born), we noticed they were having a revival. Brother R.C. and Dorothy Wigginton were the leaders of the revival. They were the same pastors who had witnessed the prophecy given to me by Brother Don James while I was pregnant with April.

We stopped and went in as a family: Den, me, a Down's syndrome child and a baby in a body brace.

Sister Dorothy stated that the lady minister on the program had taken ill and would not be able to be there. She went on to announce that in spite of this change in plans, God had surely given the message of the hour to someone in attendance. She looked with anticipation around the room for the one God had predestined to minister.

Den said, "I don't have the message, but I do have a scripture I would like to share." Sister Dorothy immediately spoke up and told Den to come and deliver the message.

We were sitting on the front pew when Den stood up to obey her invitation. Wouldn't you know that he began to preach on "God, the Great Healer!" And, there I sat with two babies that needed a touch from the supernatural God.

I began to weep. My weeping came from a place so deep within me, and with such emotion, that I could hardly see past the tears in my eyes. I tried to be inconspicuous, as I did not want anyone to see the intensity of my feelings.

Not more than two hours prior, Den had spoken to me concerning removing the brace from our baby. I could not! Now, Den had involved the Holy Ghost – and the Holy Ghost now had hold of my emotions.

When the Holy Ghost gets involved, there is almost always some action. He sure loosed His Spirit of counsel on me that night. His voice whispered to me, (in my words) "Now is the time to remove the braces."

I mentally fought back against the Holy Ghost's prompting. I thought, "No, I am afraid of what my family will think." You see, I had already been wounded by a family member's statement that Phillip had been given to me 'afflicted' because of sin in my life. They said it happened because of my 'adulterous sin' due to a previous marriage before I was filled with the Holy Ghost. Den had also been accused of "messing with my mind" concerning the healing ability of God. My mind was overwhelmed, experiencing warfare between my flesh and my spirit.

A second time, the Spirit spoke to me and said, "Now is the time to remove those braces." Thoughts raced through my mind – the answer was still "No!" This time, I feared that if I removed the braces, the congregation would think that I was just doing it because Den was preaching on healing. I didn't want to distract them or have them think I was doing it as some sort of gimmick … or at least that is what I told myself.

The third time the Spirit counseled me, "Remove those braces NOW while your faith is great. Then, when your family and friends speak ill concerning your motherhood, you can stand on this moment."

I received that counsel from the Holy Ghost. Immediately, I reached to take off the braces. Den was preaching his heart out by now. When he realized the Holy Ghost must have been doing a work in me, confirming what the LORD had shown him earlier, he shouted, "GLORY TO GOD!"

That was just the beginning of the prophecies concerning April.

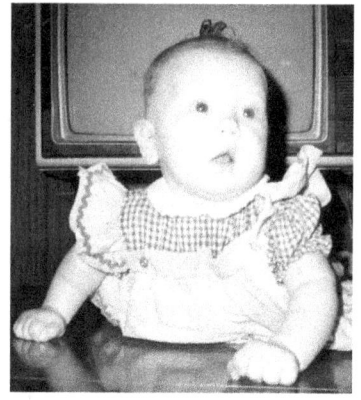

April at 6 months of age.

PEARL OF WISDOM

And make straight paths for your feet, lest that which is lame be turned out of the way; but let it rather be healed. (Hebrews 12:13)

CHAPTER 8
APRIL'S GALLOP

A pril was walking at nine months of age. She was a happy and healthy little girl. At the age of five, I took her and Phillip to Dr. Patterson at the Red Stone Arsenal Medical Center in Huntsville, Alabama, for their baby shots.

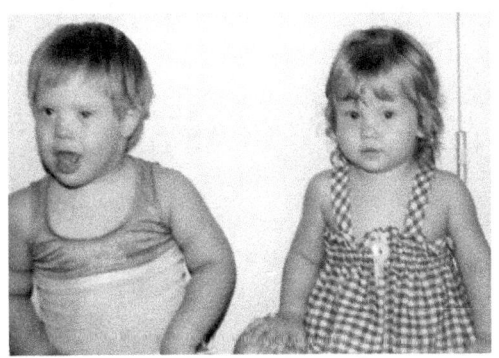

Phillip, age 2 ½, and April, age 1, getting ready to go swimming.

Dr. Patterson detected a horse-type galloping heartbeat in April. He scheduled an appointment for her to have an electrocardiogram (EKG). After interpreting the test, he advised me that there was a "little abnormality." However, he said not to worry or do anything unless she became sick to her stomach, had headaches or did not maintain appropriate growth measurements.

We practiced our faith. We prayed for her, took her to church, called for the elders of the church to pray, anointed her with oil and lived a dedicated life as much as we knew how to do.

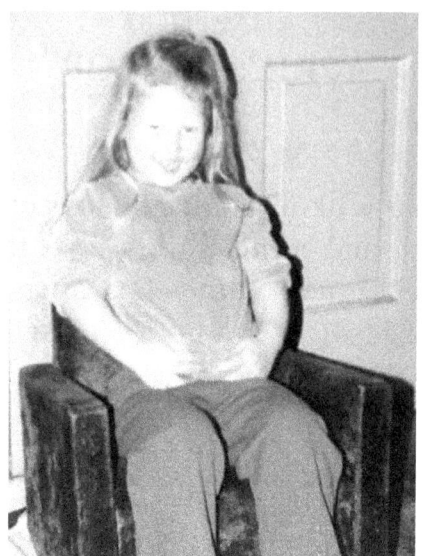

April, age 3 ½.

PEARL OF WISDOM

Be careful for nothing; but in everything by prayer and supplication with thanksgiving let your requests be made known unto God. (Philippians 4:6)

CHAPTER 9
OUR SOURCE

When Den was medically discharged, he had begun to receive disability checks from the United States Army. In addition, he also qualified for Social Security disability payments. With these two sources of income, we were able to raise our two babies and support our ministry work.

Denvil N. Keele. Relief Commander at the Tomb of the Unknown, 1970.

One day a letter came in the mail from the Social Security Administration. It was a reevaluation form.

1. How long has it been since you saw your doctor?

2. Who is your doctor?

3. What kind of medicine do you take?

4. How often do you take this medicine?

Den completed the questions as he felt God wanted him to – he told the truth. He told them that he had not seen a doctor in "five years"; his current doctor's name was "Jesus Christ"; his medicine was the "Holy Ghost"; and he took his medicine as "often as needed"! Quite satisfied with his responses, he mailed the form back to the Social Security office.

About one month later, the telephone rang. It was a representative from the Social Security office. She said, "Mr. Keele, I received your reevaluation form. Would you like to have a second chance to fill out the form?" Den responded, "No." He had been as truthful as he knew how to be. The representative did not believe him. She inquired, "Would you like me to set up an appointment for you to see a psychiatrist?" Again, Den answered, "No."

SOCIAL SECURITY ADMINISTRATION
RE-EVALUATION FORM

How long has it been since you saw your doctor?

5 years

Who is your doctor?

Jesus Christ

What kind of medicine do you take?

Holy Ghost

How often do you take this medicine?

As often as needed

She did not realize that we had pondered over that form for many days, weighing out all responses and options. We knew that one option was for Den to see a doctor just to keep the money coming. Yet, we were respectful of God and faithfully continued to believe that He would preserve Den's health if we did not lie to retain the funds. The Scripture states in 1 Timothy 6:10 that "the love of money is the root of all evil." We chose to avoid all evil, even if we had to let $1,324 per month slip away from us. If we had chosen to lie to keep the money, the money would have been gone – and possibly his healing too. (Today, Den continues to walk in his healing!)

PEARL OF WISDOM

"And every one that hath forsaken houses, or brethren, or sisters, or father, or mother, or wife, or children, or lands, for My name's sake, shall receive an hundredfold, and shall inherit everlasting life." (Matthew 19:29)

CHAPTER 10

HAVE TENT, WILL TRAVEL

Denvil studying his Bible.

We continued to serve as needed in the church at Mt. Zion. The time came when this small church desired a pastor. Den didn't know anything about pastoring. Nevertheless, since they needed a pastor, he accepted the position. We had just a few people as church members, maybe twenty. As we faithfully served this small church in the pastorate, the congregation grew to about sixty people.

Not long after his acceptance of the pastorate, Den was under the tree again. He came in to me with an announcement, "The Spirit spoke to me and told me to sell everything and go on the road with a tent revival."

My thought was, "We just got here and just got set up. All of our plans have to be interrupted. What will we do?"

So we simply mentioned about selling the house and property to family and friends. My ex-sister-in-law bought the house, property and furniture. We bought a thirty-two foot travel trailer, packed it as full as we could and hit the road with a tent, an old van, a pickup, a car and our two precious babies. A mission was about to take place. We didn't even know what a mission was, much less what an evangelist was. And, we certainly didn't know how to minister in a tent revival.

We had friends who were following construction work and currently resided in Brooksville, Florida, in Tishomingo County. They invited us to come to their town, put our old ragged tent up and try our stuff.

We preached the Word of God foolishly. The Holy Ghost showed up and began to minister to the simple little people who attended. God used them to teach us!

I think it was on a Thursday night when a man came into the tent. He was dragging his left foot and carrying his left hand in his pocket. He came up and told Den he believed God would heal him if Den prayed for him. Den reached out his hand to place it on the back of the man's neck. Unbeknown to Den, he laid his hand on a knot as big as an egg. As his hand rested there for moment, the knot just melted away.

Den told the man of how he felt the knot disappear. Immediately, Den asked the man to use his maimed hand to grasp Den's hand. The man reached out, took hold of Den's hand, and to his own surprise, he was able to grip it firmly. He began to walk with his maimed leg. He walked faster and faster until he began to hop around the tent. All the people had begun to shout with excitement by this time. Den asked the man to come back to him, God was going to open his ears. The man responded, "Too late, He already has! I can hear that piano." The whole congregation broke out in a holy roller run around the tent in celebration for the miracle received in the name of Jesus.

As the word spread about the revival, Brother Robert Swanson, pastor of the Philadelphia Church in Brooksville, Florida, came to our tent revival to check it out. He invited us to bring the revival to his church. Den accepted the invitation. There, God was faithful to continue the good work he had begun in us. We saw an unusual move of God for five consecutive weeks.

PEARL OF WISDOM

Being confident of this very thing, that He which hath begun a good work in you will perform it until the day of Jesus Christ. (Philippians 1:6)

CHAPTER 11

FAITH, FISH AND MIRACLES

Later, we found ourselves in Frostproof, Florida, pastoring a little group of people under the covering of Brother Bobby Miller. Before long, we opened up a church in an old orange packinghouse where many harlots, drug addicts and diseased people met the miracle working power of God. Many miracles took place there.

Denvil and Wanda, 1988.

Brother Den, as he was known to those who attended, saw a truth in the book of Matthew that opened a new direction to our ministry.

And Jesus answered and spake unto them again by parables, and said, "The kingdom of heaven is like unto a certain king, which made a marriage for his son, and sent forth his servants to call them that were bidden to the wedding: and they would not come."

Again, he sent forth other servants, saying, "Tell them which are bidden, 'Behold, I have prepared my dinner: my oxen and my fatlings are killed, and all things are ready: come unto the marriage.'"

But they made light of it, and went their ways, one to his farm, another to his merchandise: And the remnant took his servants, and entreated them spitefully, and slew them. But when the king heard thereof, he was wroth: and he sent forth his armies, and destroyed those murderers, and burned up their city.

Then saith he to his servants, "The wedding is ready, but they which were bidden were not worthy. Go ye therefore into the highways, and as many as ye shall find, bid to the marriage." So those servants went out into the highways, and gathered together all as many as they found, both bad and good: and the wedding was furnished with guests. (Matthew 22:1-10)

Den understood from this scripture a directive on how to prepare a feast. We are not to invite those who we expect to make recompense; but rather, to invite the lame, the crippled, the blind – the "whosoevers" – to come. And so we did!

A plan was birthed from that scripture. Brother Den and a couple of elders went fishing. God blessed their efforts; they brought back enough fish for a real feast. Den prayed over those fish, that the power of the Holy Ghost's anointing would touch everyone who ate. We held a fish fry for all of the "whosoevers" in the area.

One of the alcoholic streetwalkers, a mother of six children, came to this first fish fry. I will call her Julie. Julie ate our Holy Ghost food and took a plate to her family.

After the meal, Julie came to our house requesting prayer. Brother Den began to pray for her. She gave her heart to Jesus and then, through the power of the Holy Spirit at work in her, she was slain in the spirit on the floor. While lying on the floor, she went through the D.T.'s (alcohol detoxification). She began to vibrate all over, shaking under the influence of the Holy Ghost! When she got up off the floor, Julie was a free woman; she had been saved and delivered from all her sins. Hallelujah!

I did not know what was happening. I scooted close to Brother Den and asked him what was going on. He replied, I'll tell you later." I continued to question him, "We aren't going to get in trouble are we?" He laughed at my ignorance but my concern was real. I had never witnessed anything like that before.

When it was time for the next service, Julie came to church with her husband, her three daughters and one of her three sons. During the next few services, her husband and girls made their own personal professions of faith.

However, Julie's two oldest boys were rebellious in nature and had not come to the service with her. They just made fun of our way of worship. I paid them a visit and invited them to church. They poked a little fun at me. So I challenged them, "Do you have the GUTS to show up at a service in the old packinghouse?"

Not knowing what they were getting into, the boys accepted my dare. That night, we had a 'Pool of Bethesda' service. The boys heard the Word, went through the water, repented and were saved. Under the heavy charge of the anointing that was present, God filled them with the Holy Ghost.

That next day, the boys found themselves a barbershop and came back to church well groomed. They wanted to praise and glorify God! HALLELUJAH! They truly looked as though they were new creations. Indeed, this was the work of the mighty God we serve. The boys were never the same; they had been touched by the love of Jesus.

Later, Julie's brother also came to church. He too went to the altar and prayed the prayer of repentance. Then he stood up and told Brother Den he was born blind in one of his eyes. Brother Den prayed for his sight to be loosed. Den pulled out a church card and held it up near his blind eye. The man began to read the card. People started shouting. T. Hollis whispered to Brother Den, "You don't understand. That man can't read a lick. He didn't go to school but one day in his life!"

Opening of the blind eye was a miracle, but an even greater miracle was this man's ability to read the card. God was moving – GOD IS FOREVER GOOD!

PEARL OF WISDOM

How shall we escape, if we neglect so great salvation; which at the first began to be spoken by the LORD, and was confirmed unto us by them that heard Him; God also bearing them witness, both with signs and wonders, and with divers miracles, and gifts of the Holy Ghost, according to His own will? (Hebrews 2:3-4)

CHAPTER 12

GOD'S HAND ON PHILLIP

We had managed to raise Phillip in church, prayer and walking in the Word as much as we understood. Because God had healed Den, he thought it was only right for us to believe God for Phillip's healing too. Nevertheless, Phillip became very ill as related symptoms of Down's syndrome surfaced. His little feet swelled out of his shoes because he could not get enough oxygen for his lungs to pump water out of his body. In addition, Phillip's tonsils swelled, triggering his throat to close off and cause him to nearly drown in his own fluids.

I spent many sleepless nights caring for Phillip and listening to his terrible breathing. Finally, I called Dr. Flannery in Iuka, Mississippi, and asked him to call in a prescription to the drug store. He agreed to call it in. However, he informed me that this was the last one he could call in until he could see Phillip again in person.

I proceeded to get the prescription filled for the antibiotic. When I returned home to start the medication, Denvil was sitting in the den. He believed

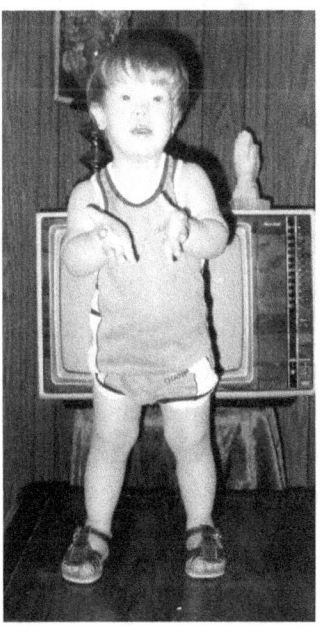

Phillip, age 2, flirting with the photographer.

that I had missed God – that I had impatiently turned to medication instead of standing on God's promises.

I was trying to learn submission to my husband according to the Scripture. So out of obedience to Den, I gave the antibiotic to a lady friend in the church and asked her to hold it for me until I could prove my faith a little longer. The lady friend took the antibiotics… and poured them in the commode. Phillip made it through the night and sure enough, he was healed. I was reminded of the scripture in 1 Samuel 15:22 that says, "To obey is better than sacrifice." My faith continued to grow.

It was during the time we ministered there at Frostproof, Florida, that Phillip had to overcome the doctors' declarations over his life – and overcome he did! In spite of the negative report given to us by the doctors at his birth, Phillip was progressing through life's major milestones. Potty training was a success. He entered school when he was five years old. We treated him like a normal child. As a result, Phillip believed he was no different from his sister or any of the other children he met.

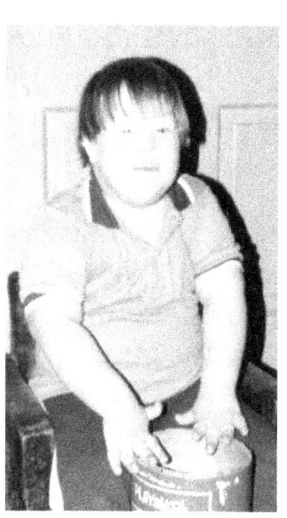

Phillip, age 3 ½, charming his Grandma Johnson in Tishomingo, Mississippi.

God's hand remained on Phillip. At the age of five, Phillip stopped me one day in the middle of a praise and worship service in Frostproof, Florida. His speech was not clear, so it took me a moment to understand what he was saying, "Corn, corn, toe and toe." Brother M.C. Collins, a minister of the church, immediately spoke out, "That's for me, I have corns on both of my little toes and they are hurting me really bad." Phillip laid hands on him and prayed. Brother M.C. went away from that service healed. Phillip was always being used by God, most of the time in such an unusual way that it was obvious it had to be God.

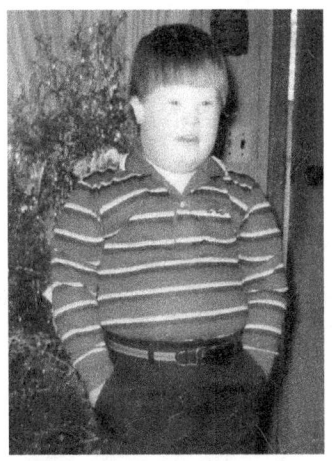

Phillip, age 5, ready to go to church saying, "Them folks need a dose of medicine."

Den continued pastoring in the old packinghouse in Frostproof, Florida, for approximately three years. This particular time of our lives provided us with hands-on training and instruction in the Word, the Spirit, the church and the people.

We experienced many things, different avenues than we could have ever imagined in the Christian world. We realized that people in the natural are often self-centered – averse to the proper manner in which others should be helped. Yes, we learned that people are just people.

PEARL OF WISDOM

"This gift [prophetic anointing] is what makes Phillip special, not the Down's syndrome he was born with." – Dr. Wanda Keele

CHAPTER 13

GOING TO THE CHAPEL

Den was asked to hold a revival on the "Foundation of a Church" for a group of people at Charity Chapel in the Crooked Oak community, a suburb of Tuscumbia, Alabama. During that meeting, God performed a major miracle!

A young mother had been disabled during the birth of her last child. One of her pelvic bones had rotated out of alignment. When she walked, one leg was at least six inches shorter than the other one. She came to Den for prayer. He instructed her to take a seat. The people gathered around to see what would happen.

Some time before, Brother Charles Strickland of Bartow, Florida, had taught us about this type of healing. We have the authority through Christ to pray for limbs and command them to be equal. (See Proverbs 26:7, Matthew 11:5, Acts 3:2.) Den received the knowledge and began to let it operate in our ministry. Personally, I was a little doubtful since I hadn't witnessed any miracle so visible before. I was eager to see what God would do.

I watched Den. I could read his countenance. He had determination all over his face. I proceeded to assist him by holding the young lady's feet. As he prayed, the pelvic bone began to move and we saw the length of her legs change right before our eyes! She began to shake under the influence of the Holy Ghost. Filled with awe and thanksgiving, the congregation began to shout and run.

However, one lady was headed outside, away from this awesome move of God. She ran through the front door of the church as fast as she could go. I sensed her fear and followed her to share the written Word with her. She became calm and received the miracle as a benefit from God.

The people were excited! They asked Den to become their pastor and he accepted. Brother Eddie Roberts, a pastor friend, took over the packinghouse ministry congregation in Frostproof and we made the move back to Alabama. Den was able to lead the members of Charity Chapel church in their purchase of a building. Before long, the membership had grown to a congregation of 120 people.

Mt. Zion, the first church Bro. Den pastored.

While there, we received instruction from God to form a Christian school that our own children might be spared from the evils of society. I received His Word as though it was from 'headquarters' and began to search out information regarding how to go about starting a

Christian school. With the divine leadership of the Holy Ghost, we were able to accomplish this great task and Charity Chapel Christian Academy was birthed.

Charity Chapel Christian Academy was a blessing to many children and their families. In addition, it assisted in homeschooling matters too. We found that in our opinion many children had been mislabeled by schools, because of how federal funding works. A child identified as having a learning problem is worth more financially to the public school system; so in some cases, there may be a financial incentive for them to place children into special education programs.

Phillip, age 4 ½, and April, age 3, practicing saying "cheese."

My mind recalls Jason, a young man, who at the age of twelve came to Charity Chapel Christian Academy by way of his grandmother. He was not able to attend school because he had a stomach problem. Doctors told his grandmother that he had a "nervous stomach." When Den and I prayed for him, God healed his stomach. He graduated through the Academy by way of homeschooling. He currently works at a sportsman shop in Tuscumbia, Alabama. One of his jobs there is to design t-shirts for the company.

PEARL OF WISDOM

Jesus said unto him, "If thou canst believe, all things are possible to him that believeth." (Mark 9:23)

CHAPTER 14

LIFE SUPPORT

On October 17, 1992, at the age of fourteen, Phillip became very ill again. His breathing was labored and his chest sounded congested. April and a friend, Joann James, took him to the hospital at the Red Stone Arsenal in Huntsville, Alabama. Immediately, the staff recognized the severity of Phillip's breathing and had him moved to the Huntsville Hospital.

Phillip, age 5, first time horseback riding.

The doctors on call there diagnosed him with double pneumonia. They informed us he would not live without life support. Yet, they also told us that if he did go on life support, he would most likely never be able to be taken off of it – NEVER. What they were telling us was that if he even recovered from the pneumonia, he would be in a nursing home for the rest of his life on life support. Without it ... he would die.

I begged the doctor to help Phillip in the same way he would help me if I were the one with the double pneumonia diagnosis. I also informed the staff that Phillip indeed would be able to breathe when he came off the life support. He was worth saving! He was an asset to our community, our church, our family and our school. We did not want his life wasted in a nursing home. Help was within reach and he deserved the best the doctors had to offer.

Finally, the doctor ordered the life support for Phillip. However, he never did comfort me or even attempt to assure me that he would do everything possible to save Phillip. I went on a fast immediately. It was a Monday evening. On Wednesday, two days later, the doctor finally had a session with me and committed to do everything possible to help Phillip.

My fast lasted until Saturday morning when Phillip coughed the life support tube out! Glory to God! I did not have to make a decision whether to pull the tube or not. God had shown up again!

We thanked God for His faithfulness and enjoyed each other's company over a good breakfast after the five-day fast. April was relieved that this ordeal with Phillip was over. Although she was twenty months younger than Phillip was, April carried the responsibility to watch out for him, out of necessity, when he was out of our sights. She learned how to lean on God through tough times like this. We were all learning.

I stayed at the hospital – afraid to leave. At about three o'clock in the morning, a little old lady, dressed in her gown, came walking through the lobby where I was sitting. I had been weeping and my eyes were red and swollen. The little lady came over to me, took me by the hand and said, "You are getting a miracle." Then she disappeared. Over the next few days, I searched the halls on that floor for a woman's name. There was not even one woman on that hospital floor, only men. I never saw her again. Although I did not recognize her as being a messenger from God when she first came to me, I came to believe that lady was an angel bringing me assurance that everything was going to be all right. I did not let up on prayer and fasting. I resolved to continue to resist the enemy, storming heaven on Phillip's behalf – until the battle was won.

After Phillip had coughed out the life support tube, his oxygen saturation levels began to drop dangerously low. The doctor did not hesitate to put the tube back into him. I went back on the fast. On Monday morning, Phillip coughed the tube out again. This time he was fine. I cried, "Hallelujah! Glory to God! Thank you, Jesus! Amen!" I did not have to make the decision; God had shown up again!

On October 31, 1992, the enemy whispered to me and informed me that Phillip was going out the back door this time, meaning the hearse would be coming for him. I began to resist the spirit of the thief that comes to steal, kill and destroy. I spoke to death, "Death you can't have him. He is going home with the family. The family is going out the front door."

I fasted again. A few minutes before midnight, I called the nurse's station and asked permission to see Phillip. The head nurse gave approval. I slipped into

Phillip's room in the intensive care unit and began to pray quietly. "Death, you can't come in here. The blood of Jesus has been pled over Phillip. He will live and not die. No witchcraft will be administered to him for the prince of witchcraft to celebrate." I began to praise God and watched the clock pass midnight.

The next day, I inquired of one of the nurses on duty whether they had lost a patient the night before. The nurse informed me that someone had passed away about three beds down from Phillip. How awesome it is to serve a true and living God who delivers His children out of the perils of life! These times of difficulty are tools used by God to make Himself known to us – to show us His true character.

When the physician dismissed Phillip the following Thursday, Phillip presented the doctor with a paper that he had colored for him. On the sheet, Phillip had written, "Thanks, Phillip." The doctor had tears in his eyes as he watched Phillip, April and I walk toward the front door and out of the hospital. Hallelujah! Glory to God! Surely, that doctor believes in miracles now.

PEARL OF WISDOM

The LORD is nigh unto them that are of a broken heart; and saveth such as be of a contrite spirit. (Psalm 34:18)

CHAPTER 15

"I SEE A BABY"

A t another Charity Chapel service, a lady, whom I will call Darlene, went to the altar. She had just had a baby boy a few months prior to that day. On her way back to her seat, Phillip spoke a word of prophecy to her, "I see a baby in your womb." The lady looked surprised and said, "I don't think so."

Phillip, age 5, trying to ride "Ole Goat."

It was obvious to us that Phillip had missed the Spirit of God. Although he was fifteen years old at this time, I was unsure whether Phillip even knew what a womb was. I asked him, "What is a womb?" He replied, "Like baby Moses was in." Well, guess what!?! Darlene came back to us with a report that she was fourteen weeks pregnant. I ask you, "Can God use a Down's syndrome child?"

Scripture discusses how those born with "special needs" in the family of Aaron were not allowed to come near to God in the sanctuary. A number of specific conditions were mentioned including: a broken hand, a crooked back, a blemished eye or a dwarf. They were allowed to eat of the holy bread, but they were not allowed to minister to God. "Only he shall not go in unto the vail, nor come nigh unto the altar, because he hath a blemish; that he profane not My sanctuaries: for I the LORD do sanctify them" (Lev. 21:23).

Thank God, in the New Testament, all of this changed drastically through the cross. The Bible explains, "Wherefore Jesus also, that He might sanctify the people with His own blood, suffered without the gate" (Hebrews 13:12). In other words, our Savior experienced what it felt like to be an outcast, so that He could relate to all of us who have 'blemishes' in our hearts and lives (and that includes ALL of us). Through the redemptive price Jesus paid, now we can ALL come into the presence of God and we can ALL be used of God. Yes, it is really true, "Whosoever will, let him come!"

PEARL OF WISDOM

For by one offering He hath perfected for ever them that are sanctified. (Hebrews 10:14)

CHAPTER 16
CODE BLUE

All was well for a while … then another peril came. At the age of sixteen, Phillip had an encounter with toxins filling his body. It made it very difficult for him to breathe. Seeking medical attention, I took off driving to Iuka, Mississippi, with Phillip and April.

Phillip, age 18, showing his dimple.

On the way, our family car suddenly just plain quit running. I pulled off on the side of Highway 72 near the weigh station in Iuka, Mississippi. Just as I pulled off the road, a man who had pulled a cross all over the world was walking down the shoulder of the road. He stopped and inquired about our problem. Without explanation, I asked him to lay hands on Phillip and pray for him because he was in trouble. The man looked at me rather puzzled and said, "I have never done that before." In spite of his lack of experience, he removed his cap and proceeded to pray.

After his prayer, I asked him to look at the battery to see if there was a visible problem with the car. He could not detect anything wrong and closed the hood. I got back in the car, turned the switch and lo and behold, the car started. April and I thanked God and proceeded to rush to Dr. Flannery's office in Iuka.

Dr. Flannery swiftly escorted us to the Iuka Hospital where they loaded Phillip in the ambulance and rushed him to Tupelo Hospital, in Tupelo, Mississippi. There, they informed me that the toxins in Phillip's body were greater in number than the saturation numbers. If Phillip was going to live, these numbers had to reverse. April and I were continually praying; we knew God was able. We wanted to see Him show up again! Phillip was admitted to intensive care. The staff worked exhaustively with him. It was evening before Den was able to arrive. Shortly thereafter, Den and April heard the code blue sound and assumed it was for Phillip. I never heard the alarm – maybe I couldn't handle it – the helmet of salvation covered my ears.

Soon, the doctor came out and spoke with us. He said they had lost Phillip at one point; Phillip's heart missed about ten beats. His liver and his kidneys had shrunk. However, he could not tell yet whether there was any brain damage.

Den asked the doctor to give Phillip three days before making a decision about how to proceed with Phillip's treatment. Based on biblical history, Jesus only stayed down for three days. The Word of God states we can do all of the things that Jesus did and even greater.

AGAIN, we stormed the throne of God. I visited the chapel in the hospital and gave the chaplain an offering. I fasted and did every spiritual thing I could think of. Thank God! Prayer worked. Ministry of helps worked. Medication worked. Soon the toxic numbers began to go down and the clean oxygen began to have dominion in Phillip's body. Our God is an awesome God!

Phillip really got one of his greatest miracles during this hospital stay. Yes, his oxygen levels returned to normal, but God didn't stop there. Phillip's torso did not expand normally. Because of this, he was not able to breathe deep enough to keep down the toxic poisons.

CPAP machines had just been developed. CPAP is an acronym for Continuous Positive Airway Pressure. One of the nurses on duty recognized that Phillip didn't breathe well while he slept. She spoke to the staff concerning the issue. As a result, the doctor ordered a CPAP with oxygen.

That device was one of the greatest things that changed Phillip's life; in fact, it changed the entire Keele family. April had not been able to sleep since she was accustomed to listening for Phillip's snoring. That was no longer necessary. Thank God! (Phillip has not had pneumonia since.)

PEARL OF WISDOM

And He took them up in his arms, put His hands upon them, and blessed them. (Mark 10:16)

CHAPTER 17
OFF TO WORK

Both Phillip and April were educated at Charity Chapel Christian Academy. Phillip received a special diploma, and April received a college preparatory diploma. She later attended Northwest Junior College and received her Certified Nursing Assistance (CNA) license.

April, age 17, graduation picture.

Phillip's health increased so considerably that, by the time he was eighteen, he wanted a job. I took him to the Windwood Inn in Russellville, Alabama, to get an application. The manager, Ms. Bradford, spoke with us and was willing to give Phillip an opportunity. She hired him two to three hours a day, two days per week. Phillip's assignment was to fold towels and sheets, sweep the parking lot and tie up garbage.

Phillip's new job was such a special occasion, even for our community. In July of 1996, Phillip was featured in a segment of the Channel 15, WHNT evening news in Huntsville, Alabama. The show was called "Positive Thinking." On that particular show, they also reported on a visit by Ms. America, Heather Whitestone, for her recent stop in the Shoals area. Ms. Whitestone had accomplished her dream of becoming Ms. America – in spite of a speech impediment. Phillip was well on his way to seeing his own dreams come to pass.

Phillip's receiving his special education diploma from Charity Chapel Christian Academy in 1996.

PEARL OF WISDOM

"Special people can exercise immeasurable faith in their lives if given the opportunity and appropriate support." – Dr. Wanda Keele

CHAPTER 18

APRIL'S FAMILY

I n spite of her medical scare as a baby and her exposure to Phillip's struggles, April went on to lead a normal childhood. She was active in school. Because she attended a small school, April even played football with the boys. She also enjoyed playing basketball and ran races on the track team. She was hardly ever on the side of the defeated team.

April, age 17.

April Sue Keele and Bradley Bogus on their wedding night.

On August 16, 1997, April married Bradley Bogus, a young man who was a classmate from Charity Chapel Christian Academy.

Shortly thereafter, April conceived our first grandbaby. Brad and April chose Dr. Bradenton Richmond to take care of her pregnancy. Dr. Richmond examined April. And just like her childhood doctor, he detected a galloping heartbeat.

Dr. Richmond was a believer in Jesus Christ. In fact, he witnessed to Brad and April on their first visit. He assured them he was not afraid to deliver this baby if we all trusted in Jesus. We all confirmed that Jesus was our 'source' and 'resource.'

From the time April was very young, she received powerful teachings on how to walk in faith. She had witnessed the attacks of sickness on Phillip. More importantly, April had experienced firsthand how God delivered Phillip out of them ALL!

April's pregnancy progressed without complication, no heart problems whatsoever. Her blood pressure and heart rate couldn't have been better. April proudly introduced us to her big, bouncing boy, Zackery Brandon Bogus, on February 4, 1998.

Zackery Brandon Bogus, age 6.

April knew how to press through to victory with God on her side. April and Brad had been blessed by God with the gift of Zackery. Again, God had proven that He is faithful.

PEARL OF WISDOM

Train up a child in the way he should go: and when he is old, he will not depart from it.
(Proverbs 22:6)

CHAPTER 19

BACKWARDS PLUMBING

When Zackery was thirty-five months of age, April became pregnant again. This time, Dr. Richmond was not able to take April as a patient because his medical partner would not agree with the care of someone who had a heart disorder. Dr. Richmond referred her to a heart specialist; however, the specialist did not know how to address her condition.

Finally, April was referred to the University of Alabama Hospital where the head heart doctor gave her the "ultimate examination." He listened to the galloping heartbeat. He saw it on the ultrasound and the x-rays. Finally, he began questioning April concerning who had done her heart surgery. She informed him she had not had any surgery at all.

The doctor proceeded to open her gown and check her for scars. He found no scarring – seeing was believing. Surrendering his stance, he replied, "Nope, I guess you haven't had surgery. Well, whoever did this to you knew what they were doing. Your heart has been put in backwards, but the plumbing is hooked up correctly."

At that moment, that highly educated man had to admit there was a God – only God could have done this mighty act and made it work – and without a scar to boot! April's frontal x-ray looked like the back of the heart; the back looked like the front of her heart. Wow! We just witnessed the prophecy come to pass that had been spoken over her approximately eighteen years prior.

"When men look upon the thing in your womb, they are going to recognize that God has touched it and they will know that God is God."

The prophecy was now at work. When a true prophet speaks, that Word will live forever! Our God is an awesome God!

April had to go to the University Hospital for the delivery of this second baby. The hospital staff was on alert, ready to perform surgery if necessary. They rolled out the "red carpet." The Bogus family was given priority treatment. Both Bradley and I were permitted to stay in the room with April the entire time. Everything went perfectly. Brooklynn Michelle Bogus was born January 16, 2001. She was perfect in every way. We are so grateful to serve a God that knows how to give us extravagant loving care while He watches over us with intense jealousy.

Brooklynn Michelle Bogus, age 2.

April came home with baby number two and continued her life as usual. She was a wife, mother and daughter. She worked, enjoyed sports and still had no trouble with her backwards-plumbed heart.

PEARL OF WISDOM

They shall not labour in vain, nor bring forth for trouble, for they are the seed of the blessed of the LORD, and their offspring with them. (Isaiah 65:23)

CHAPTER 20

PHILLIP'S HEART CRY

P hillip's heart, however, was another story. Phillip was now twenty-four years of age. His heart cried out for a soul mate, a lifelong love. He would stand in the sanctuary and weep, asking the congregation to pray that God would send someone who would love him. I told him he would have to find a girlfriend with Down's syndrome. I believed this because I didn't want him to be unequally yoked. He disagreed. He wanted a "regular" woman.

One Sunday morning in 2002, a molasses blonde, "regular" woman came visiting Charity Chapel Church where Den was still pastoring. She did not recognize that Phillip had Down's syndrome – we had prayed until his facial features were almost normal.

Her name was Elizabeth Jones. Elizabeth was older than Phillip was. She had her drivers' license and her own car. Phillip approached me and asked permission to date this young lady. Den and I agreed to let Phillip and Elizabeth go to Burger King together.

They went to get hamburgers several times. Sometimes they went to the park. They held hands, embraced, laughed and enjoyed each other's company. As we got to know Elizabeth, or "Sissy" as Phillip called her, we learned about her love for the LORD and her trust in His provision. She shared about her encounter with brain cancer at the age of twelve and her ongoing struggle to manage her diabetes. She also told us of her two previously failed marriages. Through it all, she counted on God to reward her faith. She trusted Him to answer her prayer for a happy life – she desired a Godly husband and Christian home.

One night, Phillip came to me and said, "Mom, me and Sissy want to do more than just date – we want a relationship – we want to get married."

Phillip and Elizabeth in love. Photo used by permission of TimesDaily, Florence, Alabama.

I cannot even begin to describe the array of emotions that Den and I felt. We were both shocked! I had embraced the fact that Phillip would never marry due to his Down's syndrome. But now, all of the Down's limitations just left my mind and faith had to take over. I began to 'see' this heart's desire for Phillip as a real possibility in his life. Den was worse than I was; he struggled to grasp hold of the vision of a different life for Phillip. He responded, "There ain't no way, forget that!" Of course, once Den had more time to process the shocking news, he came around and gave Phillip and Elizabeth his blessing.

Elizabeth's parents also had mixed feelings about the marriage proposal. Sarah, her mother, and William, her father, loved Phillip and knew he loved Elizabeth. Sarah asked Elizabeth if she knew what she was getting into. Elizabeth responded, "I know he has Down's syndrome, but I don't look at him like that. I look at him just like I look at anybody else. He means everything to me. He makes me laugh – he makes me happy – he puts joy in my heart." After having watched his daughter mistreated in her two previous marriages, William encouraged her to marry Phillip. He was the Christian man she had prayed for and would be good to her. What more could a father ask?

Once the shock was over, I still had concerns about the marriage plans, primarily because they did not have a place to live. Due to his physical medical history, we would not agree for him to move away from our reach. Nevertheless, Phillip persisted. Therefore, we began to brainstorm housing options for them that would allow him to marry, yet keep him close by.

A few years prior to this time, we had allowed one of April's friends and her husband to move a double-wide home onto the back side of our property. The young couple ended up getting a divorce and filed bankruptcy, losing ownership of the double-wide to the financial lienholder.

April and her family lived next door, across the yard in a smaller double-wide. I discussed with April and her family if they would consider moving into the bigger double-wide in the back and allow Phillip to live in the double-wide they had. That way, Phillip would be nearest to us – eighty yards away – right in our front yard.

April and her husband, Bradley, agreed. I made an effort to find the financial agent who held the paperwork on the bigger repossessed double-wide. However, I was not able to get information regarding the process for getting the double-wide released. Reluctantly, I had to put that idea to sleep.

PEARL OF WISDOM

The effectual fervent prayer of a righteous man availeth much. (James 5:16b)

CHAPTER 21

A HOME FOR PHILLIP

G od was not asleep though! He heard the cry of Phillip's heart – God was working all things together for good!

One day, a man knocked on our door. He introduced himself and explained that his business was buying and selling repossessed trailer houses. He was interested in the repossessed double-wide on our property. He explained that if he submitted the highest bid, he would need our permission to move it. I advised him I was not the man of the house; however, I could not foresee a problem.

Phillip's new home.

I invited him into the living room and introduced him to Phillip. Phillip spoke to him in a gentleman-like manner. I proceeded to explain our interest in this same double-wide trailer. I told him of how we had tried to make contact with the financial provider to purchase it ourselves.

I also told him how Phillip had prayed for God to send him a "regular" woman – and behold – he did! I went on to tell him that we would not let them marry and move out of reach because of Phillip's health problems. Neither did we believe in more than one family living in the same house at one time.

As the bidder heard this story, the Spirit of God within him bore witness with the Spirit of God in Phillip and me. He looked at Phillip and vowed, "If I submit the winning bid, I will sell the double-wide to you for the same amount I bid for it, no profit in my own pocket."

Two weeks later, he called. He had submitted the winning bid! He gave us the price, and we contacted our financial agent. God had worked all things together – and it was very good. We were able to purchase the home. The wedding was on!

PEARL OF WISDOM

"Words to live by: Treat people right."
Dr. Wanda Keele

CHAPTER 22

ANSWERED PRAYER

Phillip and Elizabeth, pronounced husband and wife by Denvil at Charity Chapel Church.

Phillip and Elizabeth united in holy matrimony on July 28, 2003. It was Phillip's twenty-fifth birthday. Den officiated the wedding held at Charity Chapel Church on top of beautiful Wagnon Mountain, Tuscumbia, Alabama. Below is an excerpt from a September 1, 2002, Times Daily article written by Michelle Rupe Eubanks.

As Wanda began to play "How Great Thou Art" on the piano, he (Denvil) walked beside his son to the [same] altar the two had shared many times before.

A ring bearer and flower girl spilling white petals on the red carpet followed not far behind, while Elizabeth tugged at her dress, took her father's arm and walked down the aisle.

She did not wear the strappy high heels or narrow dress pumps that often adorn the feet of brides. Instead, she chose simple, white bedroom slippers – the perfect shoe for her white satin and lace gown.

It wasn't an elaborate chapel draped in fabric and dripping with lilies. It wasn't awash in candlelight and filled with the sounds of Pacabel's [Pachelbel's] Canon in D. It wasn't a black tie and floor-length-gown affair.

It was much more.

It was a room filled with support for Phillip and Elizabeth. It was a room filled with the love of friends and family who packed the wood-paneled chapel [that was] responsible for bringing the couple together in the first place. It was a room that encompassed their entire world.

And when the vows had been spoken, neither shy about saying, "I do," Phillip took his new bride in his arms and kissed her, gently but eagerly, as the sound of applause interrupted the silence.

Having performed the ceremony, Denvil announced his son and wife to the audience, "Ladies and gentlemen, I give you Mr. and Mrs. Keele."

Another prayer had been answered.

Phillip and Elizabeth have each experienced the joy of companionship with a best friend through the wonder of marriage. Both Phillip and Elizabeth would like to have children someday. Elizabeth puts it this way, 'I don't know if I can have kids; but I know I believe in God – and He can work miracles."

Phillip and Elizabeth cutting the "big ole cake" at their wedding reception.

Their faith stands strong through the difficult times too. On February 17, 2010, at five o'clock in the morning, we received a phone call from Elizabeth. Phillip had developed another toxic problem. We took him to the Helen Keller Hospital. Then we did what we had learned to do from Phillip's previous perils – we believed in the Word of God! God once more moved on his behalf. Phillip's breathing returned to normal. He was released from the hospital on February 24, 2010. Again, I praised God for the ability to respond to life's perils with steadiness of mind and unyielding faith.

Despite the challenges life throws at Phillip and Elizabeth, they have found what we all are looking for; they have found LOVE – in all its simplicity.

PEARL OF WISDOM

And now abideth faith, hope, charity, these three; but the greatest of these is charity. (1 Corinthians 13:13)

CHAPTER 23

WELCOME BABY

B efore long, we received surprising news. April was pregnant again; number three was on its way. We surfed the Internet for Dr. Richmond and found him in Jacksonville, Alabama. April called him and explained that she needed him one more time. He accepted the challenge and made her an appointment. We traveled three hours one-way to seek a doctor of faith to take care of our new gift.

April experienced a wonderful pregnancy. Her delivery was perfect. On July 13, 2009, we welcomed newcomer, Braxton Tanner Bogus, to our family. Tanner was a healthy, bouncing baby boy.

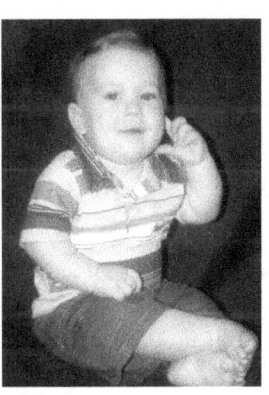

Braxton Tanner Bogus, age 1.

God did a wonderful job giving us peace throughout her pregnancy and delivery. In fact, this time, our faith was strong and tough. We did not even entertain the thought of something going wrong. Hallelujah! Glory to God! Thank you, Jesus! Amen!

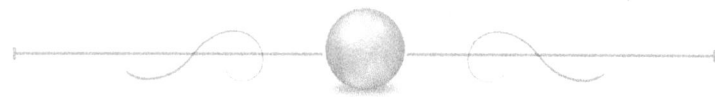

PEARL OF WISDOM

Thou wilt keep him in perfect peace, whose mind is stayed on Thee: because he trusteth in Thee. (Isaiah 26:3)

CHAPTER 24

AND NOW ...

Though strong now, my faith developed slower than Den's through the years. He was the one who had experienced the supernatural peace in his mind, soul and body when he repented that day in my apartment at the age of thirty-two.

Now, at the age of sixty-six, Den's faith is miles away from that day. Amen! He stills pastors Charity Chapel Church, Tuscumbia, Alabama. He finds great joy in spending time with our grandchildren. He is mentoring our grandson, Zack, now age thirteen, about how to hunt and live off the land. Den loves to watch Brooklynn, now age ten, play baseball. They also have special bonding time over chicken nuggets after the games. Tanner, age two, enjoys helping grandpa care for the hunting dogs.

Zackery, age 12.

At the age of thirty-two, I realized that when God touches something, it has to change. At age sixty-five, I wouldn't want to change experiences with anyone. The journey hasn't been easy, but it was so very worth it to see what

Brooklynn, age 9.

God can do when we lay our dreams, hopes and fears at His feet. I don't just know about a god; I know the one and only true God. Ephesians 3:20 states, "Now unto Him that is able to do exceeding abundantly above all that we ask or think, according to the power that worketh in us, unto Him be glory in the church by Christ Jesus throughout all ages, world without end. Amen."

April and Tanner enjoying play time.

Denvil, age 61, and Wanda, age 60.

Today, I have a doctorate degree in theology from Tabernacle College in Tampa, Florida. I am the administrator over Provision Ministry, a goods and clothing ministry to the widows and the fatherless. I am also the principal at Keys to the Kingdom Christian School in Iuka, Mississippi.

Phillip is now thirty-two years of age. He has grown into a solid man of God in his own right. He is far from that eight year old, holding fast to his faith in God to disprove the bad report the doctors spoke over him. No, he would not die at the age of eight – he would live – and live life to the fullest! Every bad report the doctors spoke over Phillip had to bow down

Phillip ministering with his father, Denvil.
Photo used by permission of TimesDaily,
Florence, Alabama.

under the name of JESUS. Phillip overcame all but one of the curses spoken against him when he was born; he has not yet reproduced in the natural. He says he still believes God for that too. Phillip stands on the Bible promise that our seed will be blessed if we believe.

> *For I will pour water upon him that is thirsty,*
> *and floods upon the dry ground: I will pour my*
> *spirit upon thy seed, and my blessing upon thine*
> *offspring: and they shall spring up as among*
> *the grass, as willows by the water courses.*
> (Isaiah 44:3-4)

Phillip received his minister's license on April 20, 1998, through United Christian Church and Ministerial Association based in Cleveland, Tennessee. He sings in the congregation, plays the drums, preaches, calls people out, tells them where in their bodies they are afflicted and prays for them. And when he prays, they are healed!

Phillip ministering under the anointing of God. Photo used by permission of TimesDaily, Florence, Alabama.

Phillip and Elizabeth now maintain themselves and live in the double-wide home that God so miraculously provided. They have their own transportation. They do their own grocery shopping. Upon their request, I help them with the management of their finances.

Phillip and Elizabeth loving life and each other. Photo used by permission of TimesDaily, Florence, Alabama.

April is now thirty-one years old. Her heart is still backwards. She is raising her three beautiful children to love and respect the God she knows. April has come to understand that the things that are to be produced in her children depend on the faith she is reproducing in them. Her seed are to be blessed, just as the promise was given to Abraham. Therefore, she is preparing for the blessing she sees coming down that dusty road. Just as we cannot see clearly through dust, we can't see our future manifested because of the veil over our faith – until we walk it out.

All I know is that my God is a great, big and wonderful God who is really worth serving! Even if there was no hereafter, knowing Jesus has made all the difference in the quality of our lives! I am so happy that we each maintained our relationships with Jesus as we passed through the perils we encountered.

Your life journey will bring different perils than ours. However, God is God. He is no respecter of persons; God will do for you just as He has done for us. In the midst of the perils, it is almost impossible to see the blessing, but when God touches it, the peril always produces a pearl. We have a string of pearls – created out of difficulties and pain – each pearl points to a wonder-working Creator who asks us to bring our perils to His feet daily.

God bless you. I pray that we may impart to you – through our story – the ability to face any situation that might come in your life. Let God touch it ... and see what He will do.

PEARL OF WISDOM

Now unto Him that is able to do exceeding abundantly above all that we ask or think, according to the power that worketh in us, unto Him be glory in the church by Christ Jesus throughout all ages, world without end. Amen. (Ephesians 3:20- 21)

AFTERWORD

By MIKE SHREVE
Founder, Deeper Revelation Books

So now you have read through Wanda Keele's first book, *From Perils to Pearls*. I pray that you have been enriched by every story and that God will move in your life just as miraculously.

Don't you think it is fitting that when John saw the heavenly city, New Jerusalem, that the twelve entrances looked like GATES OF PEARL? Surely, the Master Architect was speaking something quite symbolic when He designed His eternal city this way.

In this book we learned that the gateways to great blessing in this world often involve many pearl-like challenges – painful circumstances, difficult trials and even heart-breaking disappointments. But not only do these negative circumstances bring positive results in time (when we react in faith) – they also become portals into eternity as well. As the Scripture declares:

> *For I reckon that the sufferings of this present time are not worthy to be compared with the glory which shall be revealed in us.* (Romans 8:18)

Yes, one day, glorious "gates of pearl" will swing open for all who believe, welcoming us into such a spectacular and beautiful future that no words could sufficiently describe it.

God wants this glorious future to be yours as well. If you have never asked Jesus to be LORD of your life, now would be a great time to do so – and you too will be able to look forward to this future destiny.

All you have to do is pray the following simple prayer. It truly can change EVERYTHING!

LORD JESUS, I give You my life. Have mercy upon me and forgive my sin. Cleanse me with Your precious blood and make me a new person. I am trusting You to save my soul. By faith I receive the experience of being "born again" and the gift of eternal life. I believe that You were crucified for my sins, JESUS, and that You rose again. I also believe that I will rise to meet You one day in a glorified body when You come again for Your bride, Your "pearl of great price." Thank You, LORD, for hearing me and answering from on high.

If you prayed this prayer and would like to talk with my friends, Denvil and Wanda Keele, about the next step to becoming a true "disciple" of the LORD Jesus Christ, call or write:

PASTORS DR. DENVIL & DR. WANDA KEELE
PROVISION MINISTRY
1769 CEDAR AVE.
IUKA, MISSISSIPPI 38852
Phone: 662-424-9733
Email: wandakeele@yahoo.com

www.ingramcontent.com/pod-product-compliance
Lightning Source LLC
Chambersburg PA
CBHW070605180626
46817CB00005B/2012